INSIDE COLLEGE
# FOOTBALL

# NEBRASKA
# CORNHUSKERS

BY ROBERT COOPER

SportsZone
An Imprint of Abdo Publishing
abdobooks.com

abdobooks.com

Published by Abdo Publishing, a division of ABDO, PO Box 398166, Minneapolis, Minnesota 55439. Copyright © 2021 by Abdo Consulting Group, Inc. International copyrights reserved in all countries. No part of this book may be reproduced in any form without written permission from the publisher. SportsZone™ is a trademark and logo of Abdo Publishing.

Printed in the United States of America, North Mankato, Minnesota
012020
092020

Cover Photo: Marcus Scheer/Cal Sport Media/AP Images
Interior Photos: AP Images, 5, 14, 21, 22, 25, 43; Lynne Sladky/AP Images, 7; Jeffrey Boan/AP Images, 9; Doug Mills/AP Images, 10; Ken Wolter/Shutterstock Images, 13; Bettmann/Getty Images, 17, 27; Lincoln Journal Star/AP Images, 19; Andy Hayt/Sports Illustrated/Set Number: X27723/Getty Images, 28; Kathy Willens/AP Images, 31; Dave Weaver/AP Images, 32; John Todd/AP Images, 35; L. G. Patterson/AP Images, 36; Aaron M. Sprecher/AP Images, 39; Nati Harnik/AP Images, 41

Editor: Patrick Donnelly
Series Designer: Nikki Nordby

**Library of Congress Control Number: 2019954422**

**Publisher's Cataloging-in-Publication Data**

Names: Cooper, Robert, author.
Title: Nebraska Cornhuskers / by Robert Cooper
Description: Minneapolis, Minnesota : Abdo Publishing, 2021 | Series: Inside college football | Includes online resources and index.
Identifiers: ISBN 9781532192456 (lib. bdg.) | ISBN 9781098210359 (ebook)
Subjects: LCSH: Nebraska Cornhuskers (Football team)--Juvenile literature. | Universities and colleges--Athletics--Juvenile literature. | American football--Juvenile literature. | College sports--United States--History--Juvenile literature.
Classification: DDC 796.33263--dc23

# TABLE OF CONTENTS

**CHAPTER 1**
**TOM GETS A TITLE** .................. 4

**CHAPTER 2**
**CREATING THE CORNHUSKERS** ..................... 12

**CHAPTER 3**
**DEVANEY AND THE BLACKSHIRTS** ..................... 18

**CHAPTER 4**
**TOM TAKES OVER** .................. 26

**CHAPTER 5**
**NEBRASKA'S NEW ERA** ........... 34

| | |
|---|---|
| TIMELINE | 42 |
| QUICK STATS | 44 |
| QUOTES AND ANECDOTES | 45 |
| GLOSSARY | 46 |
| MORE INFORMATION | 47 |
| ONLINE RESOURCES | 47 |
| INDEX | 48 |
| ABOUT THE AUTHOR | 48 |

## CHAPTER 1

# TOM GETS A TITLE

University of Nebraska Cornhuskers football coach Tom Osborne had accomplished a lot during his first 21 years coaching in Lincoln, Nebraska. He had led the team to a 206–47 record since taking over in 1973. And he had won 10 Big Eight Conference championships during that time. But his teams had never won a national title.

The Huskers had come close on January 1, 1994. At the time, the Big Eight champion was invited to the Orange Bowl in Florida. It is one of the biggest and most important bowl games. Nebraska earned the invitation that season. But the Cornhuskers lost the Orange Bowl to Florida State 18–16. If Nebraska had won, the media members who voted in the Associated Press (AP) Poll would likely have named the Cornhuskers the national champion. Instead, Osborne would have to wait for another chance.

Quarterback Brook Berringer stepped in and helped lead Nebraska to the Orange Bowl following the 1994 season.

## ORANGE BOWL BEATINGS

After a dominant run from 1970 to 1972 during which they won three straight Orange Bowls, the Cornhuskers lost seven of their next eight Orange Bowl games. That included three losses to Miami and two to Florida State. They even lost three in a row from 1991 to 1993 before facing Miami in the January 1, 1995, Orange Bowl.

He did not have to wait long. Nebraska players nicknamed the 1994 season "Unfinished Business." For the second consecutive year they went undefeated during the regular season. And on January 1, 1995, the Cornhuskers found themselves in the same position as the year before. This time they faced the Miami Hurricanes in the Orange Bowl.

The game was played in front of a then-record 81,753 fans. The stadium, which was also called the Orange Bowl, was the Hurricanes' home field. Miami had only lost once in its previous 63 games there. Nebraska was ranked number one in the nation. Miami was ranked third. Just like the previous year, if Nebraska won the game, it would almost certainly be named the national champion.

The Cornhuskers had overcome many obstacles during the 1994 season. They started the season 4–0. But junior quarterback Tommie Frazier, one of the team's best players, developed a blood clot in his knee. Nebraska turned to junior Brook Berringer. But he suffered a partially collapsed lung and missed parts of two games. So Nebraska was forced to use a third quarterback: sophomore Matt Turman. Still, the Cornhuskers kept on winning all the way to

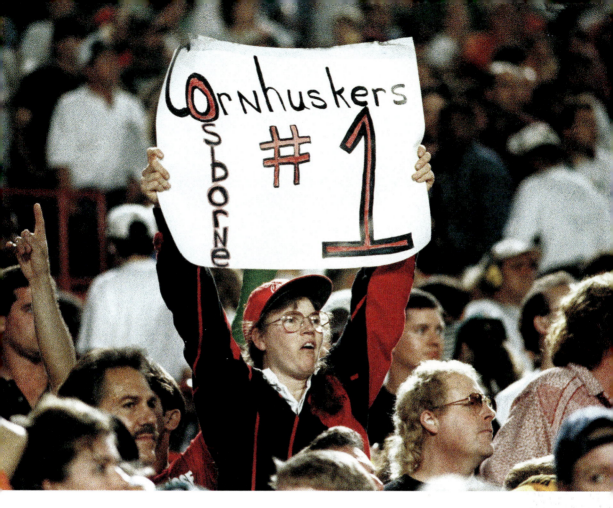

✗ Nebraska fans had faith in their team and coach Tom Osborne heading into the 1995 Orange Bowl against Miami.

the Orange Bowl. And that night in Miami, just as they had done all season, they were forced to overcome adversity.

Nebraska did not get off to a good start. The Cornhuskers prided themselves on their defense. But Hurricanes quarterback Frank Costa completed six of eight passes for 130 yards and a touchdown in the first quarter. Meanwhile, defensive tackle Warren Sapp and Miami's top-ranked defense kept Nebraska off the scoreboard in the first quarter. Even Frazier's heroic return after missing eight games was not enough. The score was 10–0 Miami after 15 minutes.

The Hurricanes were threatening to blow out the Cornhuskers. But then Berringer replaced Frazier and threw a 19-yard touchdown pass to junior tight end Mark Gilman. Nebraska went into halftime down 10–7.

In the locker room, Osborne gathered his team. He knew that Miami played an aggressive style of defense and was known for intimidating its opponents. He told his players to stick to their game plan. If they did, Miami's fast defensive players would get tired and frustrated. Then they might start to commit penalties.

## BROOK BERRINGER

In the 1993 season, sophomore quarterback Tommie Frazier had come up just short of leading Nebraska to the national title. Naturally, some fans thought Nebraska had no chance to win the national championship when Frazier suffered his blood clot in 1994. But Brook Berringer stepped in, and the Cornhuskers did not miss a beat. With Berringer under center, the team went 8–0, including a 24–7 victory over No. 2 Colorado on October 29 that vaulted the Cornhuskers to the top of the AP poll.

Tragically, Berringer was killed in a plane crash in April 1996. A statue of Berringer and Tom Osborne stands outside the Tom and Nancy Osborne Athletic Complex on the University of Nebraska campus.

✘ Nebraska fullback Cory Schlesinger dives into the end zone for the game-winning touchdown in the 1995 Orange Bowl.

But the momentum Nebraska had gained in the second quarter was quickly lost. Miami scored in the first two minutes of the second half to go up 17–7. Nebraska cut that lead to just eight points a few minutes later when the Cornhuskers' defense forced a safety. Nebraska's defense was starting to heat up. It put constant pressure on Costa and forced the Hurricanes to punt again and again.

Miami still led 17–9 heading into the fourth quarter. Osborne knew he had to do something to get his team's offense going. So he put Frazier back under center. And the Cornhuskers got back into the end zone. Frazier and sophomore running back Lawrence Phillips kept attacking Miami on the ground. The Hurricanes' big defensive linemen were starting to get tired—just what Osborne was counting on.

People were used to seeing Frazier and Phillips gain a lot of rushing yards. But it was senior fullback Cory Schlesinger who played

✕ **Nebraska players carry coach Tom Osborne off the field after they beat Miami in the 1995 Orange Bowl.**

the hero. He ran 15 yards into the end zone for a touchdown midway through the fourth quarter. Frazier tied it up with a two-point conversion pass to senior tight end Eric Alford. Schlesinger scored again a few minutes later. His 14-yard run put the Cornhuskers up 24–17. Then defensive back Kareem Moss intercepted a fourth-down desperation pass with one minute to go to ensure the victory.

Osborne had won the Orange Bowl in January 1983. However, he had lost five in a row until the January 1995 victory. The win also secured Osborne's first national championship. The coach was known for keeping his emotions under control. But those around him saw how much winning that game meant to him.

## TOM OSBORNE

Tom Osborne helped cement Nebraska's tradition of success during his time with the Cornhuskers. In his 25 years as the team's head coach, he went 255–49–3. Although he had only a 12–13 record in bowl games, few teams are consistently good enough to qualify for a bowl game 25 straight seasons. Osborne led Nebraska to three national titles: in 1994, 1995, and a shared title in 1997. He retired after the 1997 season but came back to the school in 2007 and served as its athletic director until 2013.

"You could see it in his eyes," said Nebraska's All-America senior guard Brenden Stai. "I've never seen brighter eyes in my life."

The odds had seemed stacked against the Cornhuskers all season. They had to overcome years of falling just short of a national title, and they had to do it using three different quarterbacks. But in the end, they completed the perfect season. And, to top it off, they had finally beaten Miami on their home turf.

"Going into the game, we knew we had a really solid team even though it was kind of an up-and-down year with our quarterbacks," Schlesinger said years later. "But we had a lot of character. We knew with the coaching staff we had and the game plan we had that it was going to be a good, tough game, but we knew we were going to win."

That character has been a part of Nebraska football for decades. Whether it is the team's Blackshirts on defense or its bruising running backs, the Cornhuskers' determination has helped them remain successful for more than a century.

CHAPTER 2

# CREATING THE
# CORNHUSKERS

These days, as many as 90,000 people cram into Memorial Stadium in Lincoln, Nebraska, to watch the Cornhuskers play home football games. But the school's beginnings were much more modest than that. Nebraska's first game took place on November 27, 1890, against a team from the Young Men's Christian Association (YMCA) in Omaha, Nebraska. Nebraska won by the score of 10–0.

Nebraska was a power in the early days of college football. Under coach Walter Booth, it went 46–8–1 from 1900 to 1905. That included undefeated seasons in 1902 and 1903. Nebraska did not allow a single point in that first undefeated season. But the competition at the time was not very strong. Nebraska was running out of teams to beat. So before the 1907 season, Nebraska joined the Missouri Valley Intercollegiate Athletic Association (MVIAA).

Memorial Stadium has been home to Nebraska football since 1923.

✗ **Coach Dana X. Bible led Nebraska to six conference titles and was a charter member of the College Football Hall of Fame.**

In 1911 the program's first legendary coach took over. Ewald O. "Jumbo" Stiehm coached Nebraska for just five seasons. But he made a tremendous impact. His "Stiehm Roller" teams went 35–2–3. No Nebraska coach since then has come close to matching that winning percentage of .913. Stiehm's five seasons came in the middle of a seven-year streak, from 1911 to 1917, in which the team won at least a share of the MVIAA championship each year. The program also featured its first superstar players. Senior tackle Vic Halligan became Nebraska's first All-American in 1914. He was joined on the line by All-America end Guy Chamberlin in 1915.

Nebraska is known for its great traditions. One of those traditions is Memorial Stadium, where the Cornhuskers still play their home games. The team began playing its home games there in 1923. In 1928 Nebraska and five other MVIAA teams—Oklahoma, Missouri, Iowa State, Kansas, and Kansas State—broke away and created the Big Six. The conference would change names over the years as more teams joined. But it would be the Cornhuskers' home for more than 80 years.

Coaches had come and gone through the Cornhuskers program since its beginning. All of them had kept the wins coming. In fact, before entering the Big Six, the Cornhuskers had suffered only one losing season in their history. Coach Dana X. Bible continued that

## WHY THE HUSKERS?

Nebraska's football team was not always known as the Cornhuskers. In its first decade of existence, the team was known by several different names, including the Tree-Planters, the Rattlesnake Boys, the Antelopes, the Old Gold Knights, and the Bugeaters. But in 1899, Charles "Cy" Sherman, the sports editor for the *Nebraska State Journal*, called the team the Cornhuskers for the first time. That is what people who remove the covering on corn are called. The name stuck, and Sherman became known as the "father of the Cornhuskers."

success during his eight years in charge, beginning in 1929. His teams won six Big Six titles and went undefeated in the conference during each of those six years. Nebraska's identity was built around running the ball on offense and playing tough defense. That showed with All-Americans such as tackles Ray Richards and Hugh Rhea, center Lawrence Ely, and fullbacks George Sauer and Sam Francis.

Bible's final season with the Cornhuskers was 1936. That was also the first season of the AP Poll. Nebraska finished the season ranked ninth. Bible left Nebraska for a job at Texas after that. A former army major named Lawrence McCeney "Biff" Jones replaced him.

## MEMORIAL STADIUM

Nebraska started playing its home games in Memorial Stadium in 1923. The stadium is named in honor of the Nebraskans who served in wars in the early part of the century. The official capacity of the stadium is approximately 85,000, but the largest home crowd was 91,585. That was for a game against Miami on September 20, 2014.

Big crowds are nothing new at Memorial Stadium. Neither are sellouts. In fact, Nebraska and its fans hold the record for consecutive sellouts. The streak started on November 3, 1962. Through the 2019 season, the team had sold out 375 straight games. Following a 2013 renovation, that has meant crowds of around 90,000 people for each game. When the stadium is full, the number of fans is more than the population of all but two Nebraska cities: Lincoln and Omaha. The thousands who attend the games wearing the team colors are known as the "Sea of Red."

**Nebraska players Dennis Korinek (10), Bob Smith (24), Ron Clark (23), and Dan Brown (17) prepare for the Orange Bowl in December 1954.**

Jones led the 1940 Cornhuskers to the Rose Bowl, the oldest and, some say, most prestigious bowl game. That was Nebraska's first bowl game. However, the Cornhuskers lost to Stanford 21–13. It would most definitely not be Nebraska's last bowl game. But it would be its last one for quite a while.

The Cornhuskers had only three winning seasons over the next 21 years. They made just one bowl appearance in that time. They lost to Duke 34–7 in the Orange Bowl after the 1954 season. There was a revolving door of coaching on the Cornhuskers' sidelines during that span. Jones was one of eight head coaches who had a chance to turn the program around. But none of them could change Nebraska's losing ways. Some wondered if anybody could.

CHAPTER 3

# DEVANEY AND THE BLACKSHIRTS

Nebraska was struggling in 1962. The proud program had been wallowing toward the bottom of its conference. The Cornhuskers had not been to a bowl game in eight years. But that was about the change when the team hired coach Bob Devaney in 1962.

Devaney made an immediate impact. The Cornhuskers went 9–2 and won the Gotham Bowl in his first year. The next year was even better. The Cornhuskers improved their record to 10–1. They scored almost 25 points per game, which ranked eighth in the nation. Right guard Bob "Boomer" Brown became Nebraska's first All-American in 11 years. Finally, Nebraska won the Orange Bowl 13–7 over Auburn to finish sixth in the national rankings.

The Cornhuskers and their fans would get used to high rankings. The team finished sixth in 1964, fifth in 1965, and sixth in 1966. Devaney also helped bring a toughness to Nebraska

Legendary Nebraska coach Bob Devaney talks with player Mick Ziegler in October 1968.

## BOB DEVANEY

Bob Devaney is one of the most beloved figures in Cornhuskers history. He helped lead the team to back-to-back national championships in 1970 and 1971. Along the way, he won at least a share of eight Big Eight Conference titles and tallied a 101–20–2 record. Devaney took on the role of Nebraska's athletic director in 1967, and he maintained that position after retiring as head football coach in 1972. In 1981, Devaney was elected to the College Football Hall of Fame. He served as athletic director until 1993. Devaney died in 1997.

that had been missing for years. And one seemingly minor coaching choice helped Nebraska maintain that toughness for years to come. College football ended substitution limitations for the 1964 season. That meant the era of two-way players was over—each team developed an offensive and defensive unit. Devaney gave Nebraska's defensive starters black jerseys to wear in practice. Those jerseys became a source of pride for the players. They inspired the players to work even harder so that they could be one of the Blackshirts.

Under Devaney, Nebraska became a regular in the national championship discussion. The Cornhuskers came close to winning their first national title in 1965. After winning all 10 regular-season games, the No. 3 Cornhuskers faced Alabama in the Orange Bowl. With a win Nebraska likely would have been voted national champions. However, Nebraska suffered its only loss of the season that night, 39–28.

Nebraska got another crack at the national championship in 1970. All-America senior linebacker Jerry Murtaugh led the defense. Fellow All-America senior tackle Bob Newton cleared the way for

✗ **Nebraska quarterback Dennis Claridge runs away from Auburn players during the 1964 Orange Bowl.**

the team's running backs, senior Joe Orduna and junior Jeff Kinney. And dual-threat wingback Johnny Rodgers gained 884 yards from scrimmage and scored nine touchdowns as a freshman.

The ninth-ranked Cornhuskers tied the No. 3 Southern California Trojans 21–21 in the second week of the season. After that, Nebraska was not tested until the final week of the regular season. Even then, Oklahoma could only come within a touchdown as Nebraska won 28–21. With a 10–0–1 record, the Cornhuskers were invited back to the Orange Bowl. This time, the third-ranked Cornhuskers met the fifth-ranked Louisiana State (LSU) Tigers.

At the time, the best teams played in bowl games on New Year's Day. By January 2, it was usually safe to name a national champion. Because of that, the stakes were raised by the time Nebraska and LSU kicked off. Earlier that day, top-ranked Texas had lost to Notre Dame in the Cotton Bowl. Second-ranked Ohio State had lost to

✗ **Nebraska quarterback Jerry Tagge dives over the goal line for a fourth-quarter touchdown during the 1971 Orange Bowl.**

Stanford in the Rose Bowl. That meant Nebraska would likely be national champion with a win over LSU.

Nebraska built a 10–0 lead in the first quarter. But LSU would not go down easily. By the end of the third quarter the Tigers had taken a 12–10 lead. But Nebraska did not give up either. In the fourth quarter, the Cornhuskers drove all the way to LSU's 1-yard line. When junior quarterback Jerry Tagge drove into the end zone, Nebraska regained the lead. The Cornhuskers held on for the 17–12 victory and their first national championship.

However, naming a national champion in college football was not always straightforward. There were two main polls at the time. They were the AP Poll and the United Press International (UPI) Coaches' Poll. The team ranked number one at the end of each season was considered the national champion. The AP Poll ranked Nebraska number one. However, the final UPI Poll was conducted before the bowl games, so it still ranked Texas as national champion. That resulted in both schools claiming the championship.

There would be no sharing the title after the next season. Nebraska came into the 1971 season on a 19-game unbeaten streak. Key players including Tagge, Kinney, and Rodgers were back. They were part of the third-ranked offense in the country. The Cornhuskers scored at least 30 points in every game that season. On defense, future All-Americans Larry Jacobson, Rich Glover, and Willie Harper helped command the third-best unit in the nation. They held 10 teams to seven or fewer points that year.

## JOHNNY RODGERS

Johnny Rodgers is one of the big reasons the Cornhuskers were able to win back-to-back titles in 1970 and 1971. After his breakout effort in 1970, Rodgers came back with two even better seasons for Nebraska. He was an All-American both of those years. And in 1972 he became Nebraska's first Heisman Trophy winner, as well as the first wide receiver to win the award. Rodgers was also a dominant punt and kick returner. In the final game of that season—his last ever for Nebraska—Rodgers ran for three touchdowns, caught a touchdown pass, and even threw one.

Nebraska was not seriously tested until the eleventh week of the season, against Oklahoma. But the Cornhuskers certainly had their hands full in that game. Nebraska was ranked number one, but Oklahoma was right behind at number two. Both teams were undefeated, and the winner would earn the conference title and an Orange Bowl berth. The Nebraska-Oklahoma rivalry was developing into one of the greatest in college football, and their 1971 meeting showed why. Nebraska won 35–31 in what became known as the "Game of the Century."

## GAME OF THE CENTURY

In the history of college football, it is rare for the first- and second-ranked teams to meet in a game. It is even more rare that those two teams are fierce rivals. But that was the case when Nebraska traveled to Oklahoma for a Thanksgiving Day game in 1971. What resulted became known as the "Game of the Century."

Nebraska's Johnny Rodgers opened the scoring on a 72-yard punt return. The game went back and forth. Luckily for Cornhusker fans, Nebraska scored last. Running back Jeff Kinney scored a touchdown with 1:38 left to secure a 35–31 win. That set up Nebraska's trip to the Orange Bowl and second straight national title.

"We realized whoever won that game probably would win the national championship, so it wasn't like just another football game," Rodgers said. "We were mentally and physically preparing ourselves for an all-out, gladiator-type war."

✗ Nebraska halfback Johnny Rodgers runs away from Alabama defenders during a punt return at the 1972 Orange Bowl.

The Orange Bowl turned out like most games that season. Nebraska crushed Alabama 38–6. When the final AP Poll was released, Nebraska was at the top. Just 10 years earlier, the Cornhuskers had been stuck in the bottom half of their conference. Now they had a 32-game unbeaten streak and were back-to-back national champions.

The unbeaten streak finally ended in the first game of the 1972 season with a 20–17 loss at UCLA. But Rodgers went on to have another All-America season. He also became the first Nebraska player to win the Heisman Trophy, which is given each year to the best college football player in the nation. The team finished 9–2–1 and ranked fourth in the final AP Poll. After three of the best seasons in school history, Devaney stepped away from the sidelines to focus on his role as Nebraska's athletic director. He had already been serving in that capacity since 1967. His replacement on the sideline would pick up where Devaney left off.

CHAPTER 4

# TOM TAKES *OVER*

Thanks to Bob Devaney, Cornhuskers fans got used to winning. That tradition continued when Tom Osborne took over as Nebraska's head coach for the 1973 season.

Osborne was well known at Memorial Stadium. Devaney had hired him as an assistant coach in 1967. Osborne was largely responsible for creating Nebraska's high-powered offenses during the 1970 and 1971 national championship seasons.

The Cornhuskers hardly missed a beat under Osborne. Although the team fell short of national championships, they won at least nine games in each of Osborne's first nine seasons. They also reached a bowl game after each of those seasons. Even Devaney had not done that. Nebraska won five of those bowl games. It also won at least a share of three conference titles.

Nebraska players carry coach Tom Osborne off the field following a victory over Texas in the 1974 Cotton Bowl.

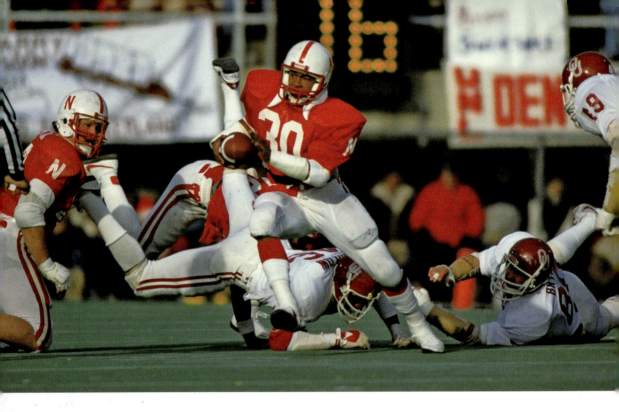

✗ Nebraska running back Mike Rozier finds space to run against Oklahoma during a 1982 home game.

And Nebraska never finished lower than number 12 in the final AP Poll of those seasons.

One of the big reasons for Nebraska's continued success was their play on the lines—both offensive and defensive. The powerful offensive linemen created lots of time and space that allowed Nebraska's skill players to shine. The defensive linemen made sure opposing quarterbacks never had much time to make a play. Numerous All-Americans cycled through the program.

Expectations were high going into the 1982 season. Nebraska ranked fourth in the preseason AP Poll. But those hopes took a hit in a September game at Penn State. Nebraska led in the final minute. But Penn State completed two disputed passes, including a touchdown with four seconds left, to win 27–24. Penn State went on to win the national title that year. Nebraska beat LSU in the Orange Bowl and finished the season ranked third.

The Cornhuskers had several important players returning for the 1983 season. When the preseason AP Poll was released, Nebraska was ranked first. The team lived up to the hype behind its powerful offense. Nebraska led the nation in scoring at more than 50 points per game.

Tailback Mike Rozier played a big role in many of those points. The senior rushed for 2,148 yards and scored 29 touchdowns. Both were Nebraska single-season records. Those numbers earned Rozier the second Heisman Trophy in Nebraska history.

Rozier was far from Nebraska's only star that season. Senior quarterback Turner Gill finished fourth in the Heisman voting. Meanwhile, senior wide receiver Irving Fryar was named an All-American.

The top-ranked, undefeated Cornhuskers met the Miami Hurricanes in the Orange Bowl on January 2, 1984. Nebraska was

## LAUDED LINEMEN

The Outland Trophy is given to the best offensive or defensive lineman in the country each year. The Lombardi Award was given to the best lineman or linebacker. Nebraska kept both awards in Lincoln during the early 1980s. In 1981 and 1982, All-America center Dave Rimington became the first player ever to win the Outland Trophy two seasons in a row. He also won the Lombardi Award in 1982. All-America guard Dean Steinkuhler followed him and won both awards in 1983.

## THE FLEA KICKER

Nebraska faced quite a scare on the way to its 1997 national championship. In the ninth week of the season, top-ranked Nebraska went on the road to face unranked rival Missouri. The Cornhuskers were heavily favored, but they soon found themselves in a tight battle. With less than a minute to go, Nebraska trailed by seven.

The Cornhuskers were able to move the ball to the Missouri 12-yard line with seven seconds left. Then senior quarterback Scott Frost threw the ball to junior wingback Shevin Wiggins near the front of the end zone. Wiggins bobbled the ball and ended up kicking it into the air. Teammate Matt Davison dove for the ball and caught it. Although kicking the ball is illegal, the referees let the play stand. Nebraska won 45–38 in overtime and kept the undefeated season intact. The famous play became known as "the flea kicker."

favored to win the game by double digits, even though it was being played at Miami's home stadium. The game turned into a classic.

Nebraska trailed 31–17 heading into the fourth quarter. But the Cornhuskers came back with two touchdowns, scoring the second one with just 48 seconds to go. With his team down 31–30, Osborne could have opted to kick the extra point and settle for a likely tie. But he decided to go for a two-point conversion and the win. After all, Nebraska's offense had been dominant all year. But the Cornhuskers were unable to convert, and Miami held on for the win. Nebraska finished the season ranked second, behind Miami.

The Cornhuskers opened each of the next seven years ranked in the top 10 of the AP Poll. Nebraska won the Sugar Bowl after the

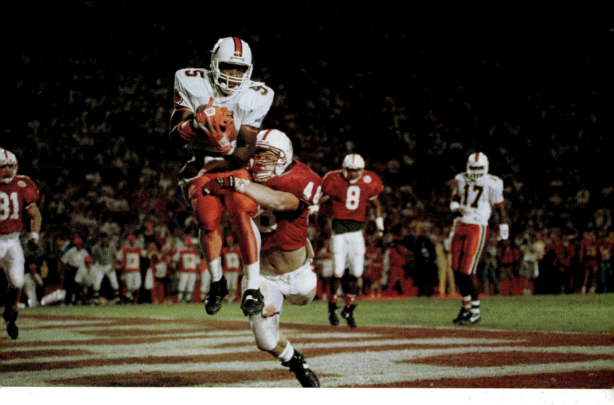

✗ **Miami scores a touchdown in the 1992 Orange Bowl. Nebraska lost to Miami in the 1984, 1989, and 1992 Orange Bowls.**

1984 and 1986 seasons. But the team then went on a seven-year losing streak in bowl games.

Some fans began to wonder if Osborne would ever lead the Cornhuskers back to the top. But he did just that in the 1994 season by winning the national championship with an Orange Bowl victory over Miami. And he was not done there. With key players such as quarterback Tommie Frazier and running back Lawrence Phillips returning, the Cornhuskers completed another undefeated regular season in 1995. The offense scored more than 53 points per game to rank first in the nation. The defense gave up just over 14 points per game to rank fourth. Nebraska beat every opponent that year by at least 14 points.

✗ Nebraska defensive end Grant Wistrom celebrates after returning an interception for a touchdown during a 1996 game.

In the Fiesta Bowl, top-ranked Nebraska faced the second-ranked Florida Gators. Florida also had a powerful offense that averaged almost 43 points per game. But it was no match for the Cornhuskers. Nebraska took a 35–10 lead into halftime. The Cornhuskers ended up blowing out Florida 62–24 and capturing their fourth national championship. It was the second time Nebraska had won back-to-back titles.

Since 1900, only three teams had won three straight national titles. Heading into the 1996 season, Nebraska had a chance to become the fourth. The Cornhuskers began the season ranked number one, but an early loss to Arizona State and a loss to Texas in the Big 12 championship game ended that dream.

Still, the Cornhuskers came back strong in 1997. Behind defensive end Grant Wistrom and quarterback Scott Frost, Nebraska rolled to its third undefeated season in four years. It ended with a dominant 42–17 win over Tennessee in the Orange Bowl. However, Michigan also went undefeated in 1997. In the final polls, the AP named Michigan the national champion while the coaches chose Nebraska. Once again the Cornhuskers had to share the national title.

## OSBORNE AFTER FOOTBALL

Cornhuskers fans admired Tom Osborne. So it is no surprise that he remained in the public eye after he retired from coaching in 1997. Osborne was elected as a US congressman three times. He also made an unsuccessful run for Nebraska governor in 2006. He then switched his focus back to the university and became Nebraska's athletic director in 2007, a position he held until 2013.

That split championship marked the end for Osborne. Prior to the Orange Bowl, he had announced the game would be his last. The stress of the position was starting to cause health problems for the coach, who was 60 years old. He turned the program over to longtime assistant coach Frank Solich, who had worked under Osborne for 19 seasons.

## CHAPTER 5

# NEBRASKA'S NEW ERA

For more than three decades, the Nebraska football program was a model of stability. Only two men had coached the team since 1962. And when Frank Solich took over in 1998, fans had every reason to believe that trend would continue.

After a fast start in 1998, Nebraska finished 9–4. One year later, everything seemed to click. Sophomore Eric Crouch became the starting quarterback. And while he could beat opponents with his arm, he might have been even more dangerous running the ball. No Nebraska player had more rushing yards or touchdowns that year. Combined with a stout defense that allowed just 13 points per game, the Cornhuskers cruised to an 11–1 record in the regular season. Then they closed out the season with a 31–21 win over Tennessee in the Fiesta Bowl.

Nebraska quarterback Eric Crouch celebrates after scoring a touchdown during a 1998 game against California.

✗ **Nebraska quarterback Eric Crouch shows his speed as he runs away from a Missouri defender during a 1999 game.**

Following a 10–2 season in 2000, the Cornhuskers appeared ready to compete for another national title in 2001. With Crouch as a senior, Nebraska won its first 11 games, each by double digits. However, a stunning 62–36 loss to Colorado in the final game of the regular season dropped Nebraska to fourth in the AP Poll.

Not all was lost, however. Crouch's performance was good enough to make him the third Heisman Trophy winner in Nebraska history. Meanwhile, when other teams lost, Nebraska jumped up to number two in the new Bowl Championship Series (BCS) rankings. That sent the team to the Rose Bowl, where it would face Miami

## ERIC CROUCH

Eric Crouch became one of the most decorated players to ever play at Nebraska. In 2001 he passed for 1,510 yards and seven touchdowns. Meanwhile, he rushed for 1,115 yards and 18 touchdowns. He even caught a 63-yard touchdown pass. In addition to winning the Heisman Trophy that year, the Nebraska legend also won several other awards.

Crouch left Nebraska as the NCAA record-holder with his 59 rushing touchdowns as a quarterback and as the Nebraska record-holder with 88 total touchdowns. However, NFL scouts did not believe his style of playing quarterback would transfer over to the professional level. Still, he was such a good athlete that the St. Louis Rams selected him in the third round of the 2002 draft.

for the national title. Although the Cornhuskers lost 37–14, the program's tradition of success appeared intact.

Very soon after, however, things began to change. The Cornhuskers went just 7–7 in 2002. It was the first time they failed to finish with a winning record since 1961—the year before Bob Devaney had taken over. Although the team came back to go 10–3 in 2003, the school fired Solich after the regular-season finale.

With that move, the stability that had served Nebraska well for four decades eroded. Bill Callahan, who had been a head coach in the National Football League (NFL), took over in 2004. But his pass-heavy offense never took hold, and he was fired after going 27–22 over four seasons. Under Callahan, Nebraska posted its first losing season in 43 seasons in 2004. The Huskers had a losing record

## NDAMUKONG SUH

Ndamukong Suh closed out the 2009 season with 12 sacks, 24 tackles for loss, and a forced fumble. Though he fell just short of winning the Heisman Trophy, finishing fourth, he took home several other awards, including the Bronko Nagurski and Chuck Bednarik Awards that are given to the best college defensive player in the nation. The Detroit Lions selected Suh second overall in the 2010 NFL Draft, and he quickly established himself as a force on that level as well.

in 2007, too, and after not missing a bowl game since 1968, the team was left out of the postseason both years.

The school turned to Bo Pelini to right the ship. He had been an assistant at Nebraska and coached the team in the 2003 Alamo Bowl after Solich was fired. Upon his return, Pelini aimed to return Nebraska to its roots as a strong defensive team.

He had some success. In 2009, Nebraska's defense allowed just over 10 points per game. That was the best in the nation. Defensive tackle Ndamukong Suh was so dominant that he became a rare defensive player to be named a finalist for the Heisman Trophy. One year later defensive back Prince Amukamara followed Suh as an All-American. However, the offense wasn't able to match the team's dominant defense, and the team finished 10–4 each year.

More change was coming for the Cornhuskers, but it wasn't another new coach quite yet. TV contracts were growing larger and larger. The college conferences, seeking to earn more and more money, began recruiting new schools. So in 2011, Nebraska left its

✗ Nebraska cornerback Prince Amukamara defends against Oklahoma during the 2010 Big 12 Championship Game.

longtime home in the Big 12 to join the richer Big Ten Conference. It was one of several teams to switch conferences around that time.

With the move, Nebraska's rivalries with longtime conference foes Colorado, Iowa State, Kansas, Kansas State, Missouri, Oklahoma, and Oklahoma State ended. However, many were excited to welcome Nebraska, with all its tradition, into the Big Ten alongside other big-time programs such as Michigan, Ohio State, and Penn State.

Many expected Nebraska to compete for a conference title right away. However, the team fell short, finishing 9–4 after a loss to South Carolina in the Capital One Bowl. That became a blueprint for the years to come. Under Pelini, Nebraska was regularly ranked in the top 25. They finished 9–4 or 10–4 in each of his seven seasons.

39

## SCOTT FROST COMES HOME

Scott Frost was just the guy that many Nebraska fans wanted as head coach. A Nebraska native, he had played quarterback for the Cornhuskers under Tom Osborne, leading the team to the shared 1997 national title. After a short NFL career, he got into coaching, where he established himself as a great offensive mind. In 2016 he got his first head coaching job, taking over for a Central Florida team that had gone winless the year before. By 2017, they were undefeated. That's when Nebraska called to bring Frost back home.

But that was too many losses for the Nebraska faithful. Before the end of that 2014 season, Pelini was fired.

"We weren't good enough in the games that mattered," Athletic Director Shawn Eichorst said. "I didn't see that changing at the end of the day."

Like the firing of Solich, however, this move backfired. Mike Riley, who had been the coach at Oregon State, led Nebraska to its worst three-year stretch in generations. The team went 6–7 and then 9–4 in Riley's first two years. His 4–8 record in 2017, however, was Nebraska's worst since 1961.

The Cornhuskers suddenly faced an identity crisis. Not only was Nebraska no longer competing for national titles; now it wasn't consistently winning. The once stable program was now looking for its fifth head coach in 16 years.

The Nebraska fans had hope, though. "This table is set as well as any place in the United States in regard to resources, facilities, infrastructure, and fan support," said new Athletic Director Bill Moos. The team just needed the right coach to put it all together.

✗ **The Nebraska football program turned to a familiar face when it hired Scott Frost to be its head coach in 2018.**

Cornhuskers fans believed they found just the man in former Nebraska quarterback Scott Frost. He returned to the school in 2018, and despite another 4–8 season while he was getting settled, hope began returning to Memorial Stadium as the Cornhuskers won four of their final six games in the 2018 season.

Nebraska came into the 2019 season with a top-20 recruiting class and a star quarterback in sophomore Adrian Martinez. However, the team's record improved by just one game to 5–7 as Frost continued the process of rebuilding one of the nation's most storied college football programs.

# TIMELINE

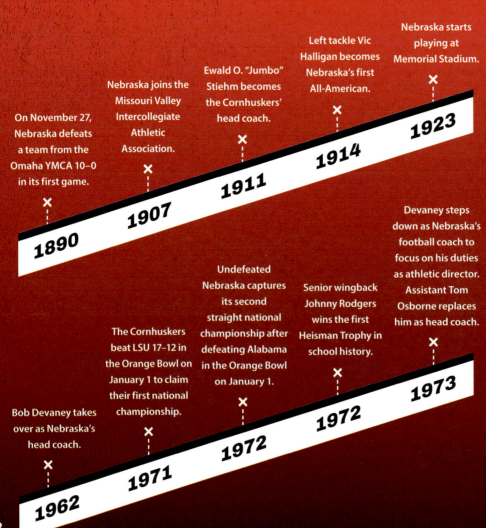

**1890** — On November 27, Nebraska defeats a team from the Omaha YMCA 10–0 in its first game.

**1907** — Nebraska joins the Missouri Valley Intercollegiate Athletic Association.

**1911** — Ewald O. "Jumbo" Stiehm becomes the Cornhuskers' head coach.

**1914** — Left tackle Vic Halligan becomes Nebraska's first All-American.

**1923** — Nebraska starts playing at Memorial Stadium.

**1962** — Bob Devaney takes over as Nebraska's head coach.

**1971** — The Cornhuskers beat LSU 17–12 in the Orange Bowl on January 1 to claim their first national championship.

**1972** — Undefeated Nebraska captures its second straight national championship after defeating Alabama in the Orange Bowl on January 1.

**1972** — Senior wingback Johnny Rodgers wins the first Heisman Trophy in school history.

**1973** — Devaney steps down as Nebraska's football coach to focus on his duties as athletic director. Assistant Tom Osborne replaces him as head coach.

42

**1982** — Senior center Dave Rimington becomes the first player to win the Outland Trophy two years in a row.

**1983** — Running back Mike Rozier wins the Heisman Trophy.

**1995** — Osborne wins his first national championship as a head coach after Nebraska defeats Miami 24–17 in the Orange Bowl on January 1.

**1996** — The Cornhuskers defeat Florida in the Fiesta Bowl on January 2 to win a second straight national championship.

**1998** — In Osborne's last game, Nebraska defeats Tennessee on January 2 and shares the national title with Michigan.

**2001** — Quarterback Eric Crouch becomes the third player to win the Heisman Trophy in Nebraska's history.

**2008** — Former Nebraska defensive coordinator Bo Pelini is named head coach.

**2011** — Nebraska finishes 9–4 in its first season in the Big Ten Conference.

**2014** — Despite Nebraska having won at least nine games in each of his seven seasons, Pelini is fired and replaced by Mike Riley.

**2018** — Following Nebraska's worst season since 1961, former Cornhuskers quarterback Scott Frost takes over as head coach.

43

# QUICK STATS

## PROGRAM INFO

University of Nebraska Old Gold
Knights (1890–91)
University of Nebraska Bugeaters,
Antelopes, Rattlesnake Boys
(1892–99)
University of Nebraska
Cornhuskers (1900– )

## NATIONAL CHAMPIONSHIPS

1970*, 1971, 1994, 1995, 1997*

## OTHER ACHIEVEMENTS

Conference championships: 43
Bowl record: 26–27

## KEY COACHES

Bob Devaney (1962–72)
101–20–2, 6–3 (bowl games)
Tom Osborne (1973–97)
255–49–3, 12–13 (bowl games)

## KEY PLAYERS

Prince Amukamara (CB, 2007–10)
Bob Brown (RG, 1961–63)
Eric Crouch (QB, 1998–2001)**
Tommie Frazier (QB, 1992–95)
Irving Fryar (WR, 1980–83)
Vic Halligan (LT, 1912–14)
Dave Rimington (C, 1979–82)
Johnny Rodgers (RB, 1970–72)**
Mike Rozier (RB, 1981–83)**
Dean Steinkuhler (RG, 1981–83)
Ndamukong Suh (DL, 2005–09)
Ed Weir (T, 1923–25)
Grant Wistrom (DE, 1994–97)

## HOME STADIUM

Memorial Stadium (1923– )


*Denotes shared title
**Heisman Trophy winner
All statistics through 2019 season

# QUOTES AND ANECDOTES

*"I thought it was probably wise to back off before someone tells you you have to go."*

*—Nebraska coach Tom Osborne at a press conference announcing his retirement on December 10, 1997. Osborne suffered from an irregular heartbeat and decided the stress of coaching was not good for his health.*

After growing up in the tiny town of Shelby, Nebraska, Curt Tomasevicz decided he wanted to play football for the Cornhuskers. Upon taking part in a tryout, he made the team in 1999 as an uninvited walk-on, and over his career he developed into a contributor on special teams. That experience helped him on his next journey. Tomasevicz went on to become one of the United States' most accomplished bobsledders. As a push athlete, he competed in three Olympics, winning a historic gold medal in 2010 and a silver medal in 2014.

One of Bo Pelini's first priorities when he took over as Nebraska's head coach in 2008 was getting the team's struggling defense back to its best. He did that by revamping the team's Blackshirts policy. He did not hand out the coveted jerseys each year until he had decided that the players had earned them on the field.

# GLOSSARY

**All-American**
A player chosen as one of the best amateurs in the country in a particular sport.

**athletic director**
An administrator who oversees an institution's coaches, players, and teams.

**bowl**
In football, a game at the end of the season where successful teams are chosen to play each other.

**conference**
In sports, a group of teams that play each other each season.

**draft**
A system that allows teams to acquire new players coming into a league.

**favored**
Expected to win.

**legendary**
Extremely famous, especially in a particular field.

**momentum**
A continued strong performance based on recent success.

**retire**
To officially end one's career.

**rival**
An opponent that brings out great emotion in a team, its fans, and its players.

**two-point conversion**
An attempt to put the ball into the end zone on the play after a touchdown.

# MORE INFORMATION

## BOOKS

Campbell, Dave. *The Story of the Orange Bowl*. Minneapolis, MN: Abdo Publishing, 2016.

Weber, Margaret. *Nebraska Cornhuskers*. New York: AV2 by Weigl, 2019.

York, Andy. *Ultimate College Football Road Trip*. Minneapolis, MN: Abdo Publishing, 2019.

## ONLINE RESOURCES

To learn more about the Nebraska Cornhuskers, please visit **abdobooklinks.com** or scan this QR code. These links are routinely monitored and updated to provide the most current information available.

## PLACES TO VISIT

### College Football Hall of Fame
cfbhall.com

This hall of fame and museum in Atlanta, Georgia, highlights the greatest players and moments in the history of college football. Among the former Cornhuskers enshrined here are Bob Brown, Dave Rimington, Johnny Rodgers, Mike Rozier, Ed Weir, and Grant Wistrom.

### Memorial Stadium
huskers.com/sports/2019/4/16/210004196.aspx?path=athletics

This has been Nebraska's home field since 1923. Named in honor of Nebraskans who have fought in wars, it is where the "Sea of Red" meets to watch the Cornhuskers play on Saturdays. Tours are available seven days a week.

# INDEX

Alford, Eric, 10
Amukamara, Prince, 38

Berringer, Brook, 6, 8
Bible, Dana X., 15–16
Booth, Walter, 12
Brown, Bob "Boomer," 18

Callahan, Bill, 37
Chamberlin, Guy, 15
Costa, Frank, 7, 9
Crouch, Eric, 34–36, 37

Davison, Matt, 30
Devaney, Bob, 18–20, 25, 26, 37

Eichorst, Shawn, 40
Ely, Lawrence, 16

Francis, Sam, 16
Frazier, Tommie, 6, 8–10, 31
Frost, Scott, 30, 33, 40, 41
Fryar, Irving, 29

Gill, Turner, 29
Gilman, Mark, 8
Glover, Rich, 23

Halligan, Vic, 15
Harper, Willie, 23

Jacobson, Larry, 23
Jones, Lawrence McCeney "Biff," 16–17

Kinney, Jeff, 21, 23, 24

Martinez, Adrian, 41
Moos, Bill, 40
Moss, Kareem, 10
Murtaugh, Jerry, 20

Newton, Bob, 20

Orduna, Joe, 21
Osborne, Tom, 4–6, 8–11, 26, 30–31, 33

Pelini, Bo, 38–40
Phillips, Lawrence, 9, 31

Rhea, Hugh, 16
Richards, Ray, 16
Riley, Mike, 40
Rimington, Dave, 29
Rodgers, Johnny, 21, 23–25
Rozier, Mike, 29

Sapp, Warren, 7
Sauer, George, 16
Schlesinger, Cory, 9–11
Sherman, Charles "Cy," 15
Solich, Frank, 33, 34, 37, 38, 40
Stai, Brenden, 11
Steinkuhler, Dean, 29
Stiehm, Ewald O. "Jumbo," 14
Suh, Ndamukong, 38

Tagge, Jerry, 22–23
Turman, Matt, 6

Wiggins, Shevin, 30
Wistrom, Grant, 33

# ABOUT THE AUTHOR

Robert Cooper is a retired law enforcement officer and lifelong football fan. He and his wife live in Seattle near their only son and two grandchildren.